The Defeat of the Cyber Bully

Written by Ben Halpert
Illustrated by Taylor Southerland

Text copyright ©2011 Ben Halpert
Illustrations copyright © 2011 Savvy Cyber Kids, Inc.
ISBN-13: 978-09827968-4-9 (Hardcover)
978-14895250-4-8 (Paperback)
Library of Congress Control Number: 2011912436
Published by: Savvy Cyber Kids, Inc., Atlanta, GA

To the children of the world, you
are not what others call you. You are
what you want to be. So dream
big and follow your dreams.

To my wife and children,
for making every day a gift.

—Ben Halpert

<3

—Taylor Southerland

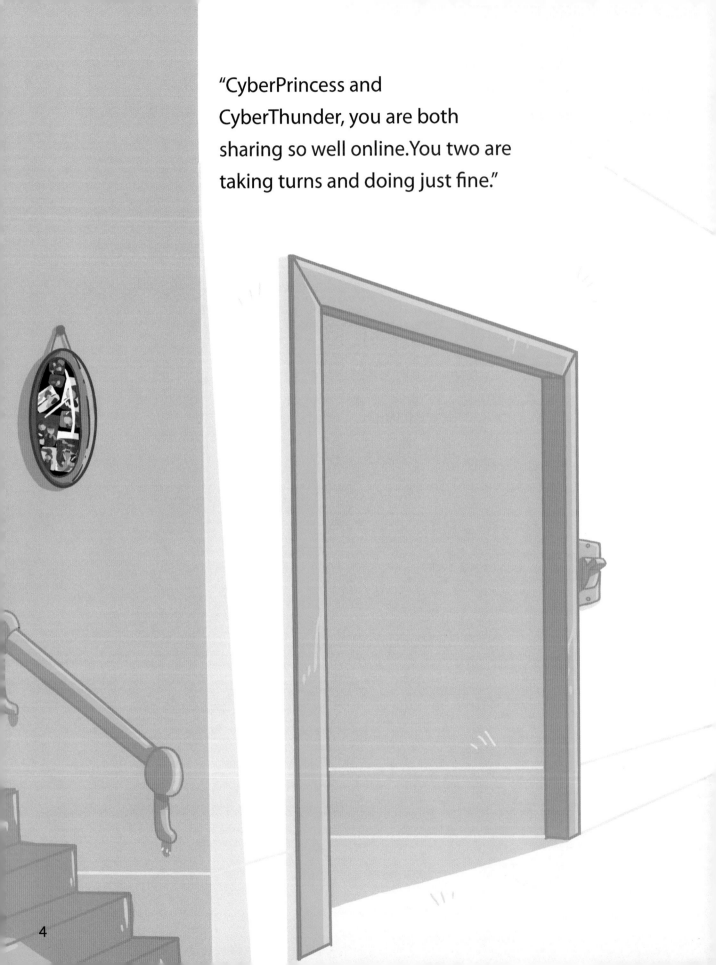

"CyberPrincess and CyberThunder, you are both sharing so well online. You two are taking turns and doing just fine."

"Thank you mom," said CyberPrincess and CyberThunder with delight. "We are planning our next move in the game and trying with all of our might."

CyberPrincess said sadly, "Another player is being mean."
"They are not on our team."

"Mom," said Tony, "someone is not being nice."
"They are saying bad things, not once but twice!"

"We typed 'Please stop', but it was like talking to a rock!", exclaimed Emma.

Emma said, "They called me ugly, gross, and slow."
Tony offered, "This is when we think about what we have learned and go with the flow."

Tony added, "That cyber bully just kept talking mean and did not stop. I used the program settings to put on a block."

Tony said, "The best thing for us to do is ignore the meanie.
When we don't respond, they feel very teenie."

Emma questioned, "Tony, is this like the time those kids were not talking nice to us on the playground?"
"Yes, some kids can be mean even with other children and parents around."

Mom said, "You two are such quick learners."
"Don't forget to tell someone you trust: like grandma,
grandpa, your teacher or me. An adult can be firmer."

Tony added, "And when you are at school, just telling your teacher is super-cool."
"Your teacher will help you and tell you to not talk to that fool."

Mom said, "When you see someone else being bullied,
you need to step up and tell the same people you trust; so
that bully will just end up being a bust."

Emma questioned, "But what if the dirty and mean talk does not stop? Can we just clean her up with a mop?"

Tony added, "Making sure whoever is talking
mean stops is a must.
That is why we always tell someone we trust!"

"That is right," mom said. "We cannot always make mean people stop.
But one day they will just be a big flop."

"So we need to pick a new activity or game. Ignoring the bully will simply put them to shame?" Asked Emma.

"Yes Emma. When I was your age," mom explained, "my parents taught me how to be. They told me that sticks and stones may break my bones but words will never hurt me."

"Sticks and Stones?" Emma asked. "Not breaking my bones?"
"That is right Emma," mom chuckled. "Remember when you two were playing with sticks? And accidentally one of you got hit?"

Mom continued, "It hurt for a minute but then you felt better.
Words can be mean, but they are only made of letters."

"But what if they do not stop?" Emma inquired.

"What if they follow me from the left, right, bottom and top?"

"Ignore the mean words, because that is what they are," Tony added.

"We can choose a new activity, and our wise choice will make us go far."

Mom said excitedly, "You kids are so smart!
You know what to do right from the start."

Mom added, "You have great friends.
So the fun never ends."

Emma and Tony shouted, "Let's play the
Savvy Cyber Kids way.
Always safe and protected online every day!"

Download free activity sheets and a lesson plan at
www.savvycyberkids.org

About Savvy Cyber Kids

The mission of Savvy Cyber Kids, a 501(c)(3) nonprofit organization, is to teach kids safety before they go online. Utilizing traditional learning tools, such as children's picture books, Savvy Cyber Kids focuses on preparing children to be more cautious when going online. Savvy Cyber Kids focuses on engraining security awareness and ethics into the minds of preschool aged children. Targeting children at the preschool level will enable appropriate decision making to be second nature as the child matures surrounded by a world filled with interactive technology.

Made in the USA
Lexington, KY
18 April 2014